# *Milo and Meg are Solid*

by Peter Wick

**Azzurri Publishing**



Cover image:

Image by Larisa Koshkina from Pixabay

Peter Wick is a writer, actor, film director, and sometimes a standup comedian.

_Milo and Meg are Solid_ is Peter Wick's first book for kids. Peter is not a kid, but he sure acts like one a lot of the time. Just ask the confused grown-ups he's always talking to.

-Special thanks to J.D. Evans, the only 12 year-old who voted on the title (from three options) as well as the back-cover write-up. His instincts were perfect both times.

*Part One*

1

"Pothole!" Meg said

"I know where the pothole is," said Milo, jumping across the hole on the ground.

"Okay, I won't tell you next time."

Thwack!

Milo stumbled into the second pothole and flailed awkwardly to the ground.

"Ow! Geez!"

"Nice one," Meg said, smiling her sarcastic sideways smile.

Meg is twelve and her brother Milo is thirteen. They were hurrying down the hill toward the street to their house.

"Come on," Meg said. "We're late. Mom and Dad will be suspicious this time."

"We'll be fine," said Milo, moving with a limp and grunting with pain as he walked.

The city of August isn't the biggest city or the coolest city, but Milo and Meg had discovered something in the city of August that they did not understand.

3

They had not told anyone yet.

They wondered if they were the only ones who knew.

"Besides," Milo said, "it's never later here than it was when we went in. No time passes."

"I know that," Meg said.

"So...what are you worried about?"

Meg looked over at Milo and rolled her eyes. "I'm worried that you won't be able to keep your mouth shut.

"I won't say anything," Milo protested. "I haven't said anything ever. Why would I start now?"

"This time was different," Meg said.

"I won't say anything."

"Okay."

Milo and Meg walked in silence for a moment.

Finally, the hill spilled out onto the street and they were almost home.

"Hi Meg! Hi Milo! Dinner's almost ready, and your mom's about to walk in the door."

"Hi Dad."

"Hi Dad."

Milo and Meg ran up the stairs. They hurried into Milo's room and closed the door.

Milo sat on the edge of the bed and Meg sat on the half-broken chair.

They looked at each other.

"What are we going to do?" Meg asked.

Milo thought for a minute. He looked at this sister and looked away.

"We have to go back after dinner," he said.

Meg nodded. "And what do we tell Mom and Dad?"

"Um…tell them we left some homework at Clarence's house."

When they came downstairs for dinner, Milo and Meg did their best to act casual and relaxed.

"Hello Sweeties," Mom said the way she always does, hugging Meg. She reached to hug Milo, but he had learned to squirm out of the hug before it happened.

"Hi Mom."

"Hey."

"Well, you would not believe the big new client we locked up today," Mom said. "…Ramsey Fisher."

"Who's Ramsey Fisher?" Meg asked.

"Who's Ramsey Fisher?! Who's Ramsey Fisher?!! Only the richest man in the whole town of August! And…he dropped his old lawyer and hired our law firm today!"

Milo and Meg looked at each other and mustered up as much fake enthusiasm as they could.

"Cool!" Milo said.

"That's awesome, Mom," Meg said, failing to hide her sarcasm.

"Well, here it is."

Dad came from the kitchen and placed a pot on the table. "My masterpiece!" He said.

The family sat around the table, happily slurping spoonfuls of their dad's masterpiece.

"Well," Dad said. "Did you learn anything today? Or has our middle school failed us once again?"

There was an awkward silence.

"Just makes my job that much harder," Dad said. He looked over at Mom. "Middle school students show up in my High School classes at the start of each year, with nothing. They didn't learn anything in all of middle school."

"I learned that if you spend a whole year in space," Meg began, "you better exercise, or the weightlessness will make your muscles go soft."

"Well now," Mom reacted. "That's something you don't learn every day!"

"Very interesting," Dad said. "And what about the trip to Mars, then?"

"Well," Meg answered, "the trip to Mars was supposed to take about a whole year, but now Scientists think they may have shortened that to about three months. But even after you get there you have the problem of Mars gravity. It's only a third of

Earth's gravity. If you want to return to Earth and still feel at all normal, you're going to have to exercise a lot, you know...like, A LOT!"

This time there was a respectful stunned silence. Milo, Mom and Dad all looked at each other.

"Milo," Dad said, "What do you have to say about all this?"

"I say we put her on a spaceship to Mars as soon as possible."

Meg playfully hit her brother on the shoulder.

"Hey, now!" Mom scolded. "You two stop needling each other!"

"Mom!" Milo objected, "It's a joke!"

"But Meg doesn't know that!"

Meg rolled her eyes. "Right! I have no idea what a joke is."

As they finished dessert, feeling relaxed and full, Milo decided to take the leap.

"Oh crap!" he shouted.

"Milo! Language!" Mom said.

"Sorry! Sorry!"

"So why all the excitement?"

"I left my backpack at Clarence's."

"Oh no," Mom said. "Anything important in it?"

"Homework. I have a test tomorrow."

Meg turned to Milo and tried her best to act upset. "I gave you my science homework. Don't tell me you left that at Clarence's too."

"It's in the backpack," Milo said.

"Genius!" Meg rolled her eyes sarcastically.

"Meg!" Mom scolded. "Don't be so hard on your brother."

"Yeah," Milo said, "show some respect."

"You have to earn respect," Meg replied.

"Careful you two." Dad added. "What have we told you both about getting along with each other?"

Milo dropped his spoon into the empty ice cream bowl. "I have to go back. It'll just take a few minutes."

"That's not necessary," said Mom. "I'll call his mom Jeanie. Maybe they can bring it by."

"No, I think I should go get it," said Milo. We were playing with some stuff I had in there. I want to make sure it's all put back in there."

"I should go too," Meg said. "Einstein here might forget my homework."

"Well..." Mom trailed off and no one said anything for a minute.

"Let's get it over with." Milo scooted his chair back from the table and stood up.

Meg did the same. "Alright, let's go."

"Don't be too long," Mom said.

Milo tried to reassure her. "Don't worry. We'll be right back."

Together, Milo and Meg walked casually to the door, opened it, and walked out into the cool evening breeze. They closed the door behind them and quickly began running.

They ran down the pathway through the front yard and were quickly out on the street.

"Come on," Milo said.

"What if we're already too late?" asked Meg.

"What do you mean?"

"We've been in the normal world for an hour. How much time passed in Icarus?"

"How should I know?"

"I'm not really asking," Meg said. "It's a rhetorical question."

"What in the H - E - double-hockey-sticks is a rhetorical question?"

Then, in her best Mom-voice, Meg said, "Milo! Language!"

They reached the bottom of the hill that sloped up toward the small but thick grove of trees.

They climbed up. Meg slipped backwards trying to make it up the hill. Milo reached his hand down to hers and helped pull her up.

At the crest of the hill Milo and Meg felt hidden from the world.

Surrounded by trees, they took a moment to settle their nerves.

This is the place that no one else knew about. Here, at the top of the hill, hidden by this grove of trees, Milo and Meg had discovered something that they could not even begin to describe.

Well," Meg said. "Let's turn ourselves into drawings."

"Okay."

They turned and walked to two trees that stood next to each other. The trees were less than twelve inches apart. To anyone walking by they looked like any two trees among the dozens in the grove.

Milo looked quickly toward his sister before squeezing between the trees. He turned sideways, edged his left foot in first, then quickly moved through the small opening.

Meg followed, also squeezing between the trees.

For a quick moment everything was dark.

Then bright white.

Then they could see.

The first time they had arrived in Icarus, a few weeks earlier, panic quickly came over both Milo and Meg.

Still feeling like your normal self, then looking down and finding yourself to be a drawing can cause shock and confusion.

The second time they came they barely had time to think about it before a large winged creature swooped down out of the sky and tried to attack them.

This time they knew better.

They ran quickly along the edge of the watercolor forest to Nannette's small hut, knocked on the door, and nearly dove into the hut as Nanette opened it.

"You're back! Thank goodness!" Nanette said, closing the door as quickly as she had opened it. "We were afraid we wouldn't be seeing you again."

"Of course you would see us again," Meg said. "Why wouldn't you?"

"Someone's been erasing us!" Nanette spat the words out angrily.

"Erasing…" Milo looked shocked.

"Look at that mountain in the distance." Nannette pointed out the window. Her anger made her shake slightly. "This morning the peak was gone. Missing. I looked out this here window and the top of the mountain just weren't there no more. Craziest thing I ever did see! Then this afternoon it was back, completely redrawn, taller than before, some of it with color, some black and white. You could'a kicked me in the head with a pair o' snow shoes and I wouldn'ta been any more shocked."

Nanette paused. She turned up the heat under a pot of tea.

"And Wolf…"

"Wolf?" Meg sounded worried.

"I don't know where he is. I think he was erased. We're all so worried."

"Tell us what we can do to help," Meg said.

Nanette looked over at her. "We hoped you would have some ideas. I mean, you come from the solid world. You are constant."

Milo and Meg shared a silent look at each other.

"Have some tea," Nanette said, setting a cup in front of each of them"

Meg looked at the cup for a moment. It was a drawing of a cup, not a real cup.

Everything in Icarus was either a drawing or a painting. Milo sipped his tea and thought about this; the watercolor forest outside...the blues, greens, reds, and yellows.

In here, though, in Nanette's hut, everything was pencil lines.

Pencil lines can be erased.

Meg picked up her cup and looked at the swirling steam that rose from the hot tea.

A thin pencil line of steam seemed to draw itself up out of the cup and into the air.

How can this be, she thought, as she raised the cup to her lips and sipped.

It tasted enough like tea, Meg thought, although there did seem to be a lingering aftertaste of pencil lead.

Milo stood up from the table and paced back and forth.

"How can we be here?" he asked. "How is this real?...IS it real?"

Nanette grabbed Milo's arm and spun him around.

She looked Milo in the eye.

"Look at me!" Nanette said.

Milo looked.

Nanette's nose had the faintest pencil lines shaping its tip. It was shaded a very subtle gray where the light from the lamp across the room turned into shadow.

"Touch my nose," Nanette demanded.

Meg set her cup on the table and walked to where Milo and Nanette stood.

"Touch my nose," Nanette repeated.

Meg coughed slightly. "That's definitely something you don't want to hear a person say, in most situations."

Milo lifted his hand.

Gently, he let his finger touch the pencil lines that formed the tip of Nanette's nose.

He could feel the edge of her nose. He could feel the not-quite point of the tip. Nanette's nose was real.

"You two are solids," Nanette said. "You come from the solid world. You can go back to the solid world. You have flesh and blood. You have intelligence."

Meg couldn't stop herself. She rolled her eyes sarcastically. "Well," she said, "'intelligence' might be going a little too far."

Milo playfully smacked his hand into Meg's shoulder.

They shared a quick smile.

"You must help us survive," Nanette said.

"What can we do, though?" Milo asked.

"First you must help me find my Wolfy. Then maybe we can find our lost friends."

"There are more of you?"

"We are a community. There are many of us, but I might be the only one free right now. And," Nanette continued, "you must find The Artist."

"Hm? The Artist?" Meg scrunched up her face in confusion.

"Someone is drawing us," Nanette continued. "Someone has created us, and that someone can also erase us."

Nanette caught her breath for a moment,

"I want my son Wolf back," she said. "Find the Artist. Tell him how important it is. The Artist does not know that we are real. The Artist thinks we are just drawings, painted people, landscapes, but we are real. We think and feel...tell The artist what he has done."

Nanette turned away from Milo and Meg and left the room.

Meg looked at her brother.

Milo shrugged. "Whose crazy fantasy is this, yours or mine?" he asked.

"I blame you," Meg said.

"Oh, thanks so much."

4

As brother and sister, Milo and Meg seemed to share thoughts. They knew each other the way no one else knew either of them. Even their own parents did not understand them the way they understood each other.

Sometimes it was as if they shared a brain, like they were twins, even though they were a year apart. They could look at each other and communicate without saying a word.

The first time Milo and Meg had discovered the strange portal into Icarus, between the two trees, was about a week earlier.

It was an accident.

They had been at the park kicking a soccer ball with Clarence and Jackson.

They were playing a small game of 2 on 2.

Milo was always amazed by his sister Meg. He never doubted her. Even though she was a year younger, she was as quick with her feet as any of the boys.

Clarence and Jackson knew it too. Playing against Milo and Meg was an equal challenge.

Using their backpacks to mark where the goals were, Meg scored the 8th goal to tie the game.

First to ten wins.

Clarence and Jackson had jumped out to the lead at 8 – 5. Milo and Meg were a little frustrated, but they trusted each other.

Together they stepped up their game.

Milo scored the $6^{th}$ and $7^{th}$. Then Meg dribbled circles around Clarence and Jackson, passed to Milo, who saw the genius run his sister was making, and passed the ball forward between Clarence and Jackson. Meg met the ball on the run, and easily tied the game.

Clarence and Jackson were good too, though, and quickly scored a $9^{th}$.

Game point.

...Not if Meg had anything to say about it.

Another brilliant dribble and pass from Meg gave Milo a chance to tie it at 9.

Then, in a moment of pure genius, Meg lifted the ball gently up into the air with her foot. Clarence and Jackson watched helplessly as it sailed just over them, bent back down to the ground as if being controlled by a remote control, and bounced, untouched, between the two backpacks.

Goal!

10 to 9. Milo and Meg won.

The boys all shook their heads and gave Meg a series of respectful fist bumps and high fives.

"I guess I better go," Clarence said.

"Me too," sighed Jackson.

"Alright, see you tomorrow," Milo said.

"See you," said Meg, and they all turned to go their different ways home.

To get to their street, Milo and Meg always took the hill with the ridge of trees.

They walked up the hill without saying anything for a minute. The silence wasn't awkward. They didn't always feel a need to talk. Silence was okay, but neither of them could resist the urge to turn semi-awkward silence into a chance to be sarcastic.

"How bad did you fail your spelling test? "Milo asked.

"I didn't fail," Meg said. "How bad did you fail history?"

"I aced it," Milo lied.

"You're lying," Meg said.

"I aced it. I swear."

"I'm going to find it," Meg said, reaching for the zipper of Milo's backpack.

"Hey! Leave my backpack alone," Milo yelled, twisting away from his sister.

She closed her fingers on the strap just as he twisted away, and Milo's backpack came off his back.

"Ha!" Meg crowed.

"Hey!"

Meg ran away up the hill. Milo chased after her.

Meg didn't really have a plan. She ran behind a tree and tossed Milo's backpack between two trees that were less than 12 inches apart.

Milo came running up behind his sister, but something made him stop.

Meg was looking at the ground between the two trees. She looked at Milo and looked back at the ground.

Milo did not understand the expression on his sister's face. It was an expression he had not seen before.

"Your backpack disappeared," Meg said.

Milo half-laughed.

Then he looked at her and scrunched up his face. Then he shook his head. "Nice try," he said, and moved around the tree on the left to look behind it.

Meg did not move.

Milo walked all the way around both trees. He circled back around to Meg. He looked left and right. He went back around the tree the opposite way.

He stood and looked at Meg.

"Where is it?" he asked.

Meg turned to him. Her face was serious. "It disappeared," she said, sounding half apologetic. "I threw it right there, and it never hit the ground. It disappeared."

"Where?"

"Right there," she said, pointing to the narrow space between the two trees.

Milo rubbed his eyes.

He struggled to decide if his sister was joking. He decided to step between the two trees himself.

As he did...he disappeared.

"Milo!" Meg screamed.

Her scream echoed off the emptiness of the surrounding trees.

She turned. She wasn't looking at anything. She just turned.

She turned back.

She knew she had no choice. She had to go after him.

She did it quickly, the way you do any scary thing quickly. She just jumped between the trees and squeezed her way through.

…And found herself in the strangest world she had ever been in.

It was not the strangest world she had ever seen, because everyone has seen drawings before.

Finding yourself IN a drawing, though, is a new and bizarre experience.

"Meg!"

She turned at the sound of Milo's voice, but what she saw made her brain do a somersault.

It was her brother…except that it wasn't.

He was a pencil drawing, mostly black and white, but he was wearing a shirt that was painted a faint watercolor red. His pants looked like they had been haphazardly and quickly painted blue.

"Come here. Look at this," he said.

She walked. She felt mostly normal. Was she thinking clearly? Was this drawing of Milo really Milo? She wasn't sure of anything.

As she stepped alongside her brother, she looked out in the direction he was looking and saw the most bizarre battle she had ever witnessed.

Creatures flew overhead, carrying spears, lances, bows and arrows. They were odd, scaly flying creatures, with sharp angles to their faces.

They swooped and dove through the air, seeming to attack something on the ground. Fires raged on the ground below them.

Then Meg could finally see who these creatures were battling. On the ground were normal mortal humans. That is, they almost looked human. They battled bravely against their flying attackers, but most of them seemed helpless against the flying creatures' attacks.

Milo and Meg were so surprised and awestruck by what they saw that they did not notice a spear flying silently through the air toward them.

It hit the ground just inches from Milo, and the shock of what was happening hit them both instantly.

Milo turned and ran deeper into the thick forest behind them. Meg ran after him, not sure what to feel or what to think.

Milo collapsed into a thick collection of bushes. Meg almost landed on top of him.

Together they tried desperately to calm themselves.

A moment of silent panic passed, their eyes darting left and right.

Then Milo pushed his sister off of him.

He rolled over, afraid to stand up right away.

He looked around to check the safety of their surroundings.

"Let's get out of here!" He said urgently.

"Let's" his sister echoed.

Milo crawled close to the spot where they entered, and moved through what looked to Meg like just another clump of bushes.

He disappeared.

Megs eyes widened with new panic as she found herself in this world alone.

Another silent spear stabbed menacingly into the ground near her, and her heart raced. She crawled to where she thought Milo had just disappeared, and…

…Suddenly…

…She was back in the regular world.

Meg didn't usually show obvious affection for her brother. She liked to express how much she loved him by teasing him. She hid her love behind sarcasm. She was surprised then, understandably, to find herself giving Milo a giant hug.

They held each other for a moment and then let go of each other.

"Next time you go in there," Meg said, the sarcasm slowly finding its way back into her voice, "I'm leaving you in there."

"Nice to know my sister has my back."

They turned and walked down the hill to their street.

The next morning, as they walked to school, Milo finally worked up the nerve to ask, "Was I dreaming it?"

"No," Meg said. "It happened."

They walked silently.

Eventually Milo broke the silence with, "Do we go back and take another look?"

Meg rolled her eyes. "We barely got out alive."

They walked silently a little longer.

Then Meg said, "Yes. We have to go back sometime."

That entire week, Milo and Meg lived their lives in what seemed to others like a normal way. Their friends at school didn't know. Their parents didn't know. No one suspected anything.

The truth, though, was that they had been visiting Icarus daily, stepping into the world briefly, adapting their dis-believing minds to the pencil and watercolor reality they found themselves in. They were also adjusting their bodies to a new balance as pencil-drawings.

With each visit they also became more involved.

They had met Nanette and Wolf. They learned about the battle going on with The Gorts, which is what Nanette and Wolf called their flying attackers.

So far Milo and Meg had managed to avoid being a part of any battles themselves.

Each time they returned to the regular world they struggled to adjust back.

They struggled to get their heads around the lack of time that passed, that no time at all had passed in the real world, no matter how long they spent in Icarus.

And now they were in Nanette's hut, sipping tea and being asked to find the Artist responsible for all of this.

This time, as they stepped back into the normal world, they couldn't think of anything to say to each other.

Their mom and dad didn't know what to think about their silence at dinner.

"Tell us something from school today," Mom said.

"Well…" Meg was trying her hardest. "Milo forgot how to add, and got everything wrong on his math test."

"Meg bombed a history test, because she thought the American Revolution happened during the Roman Empire."

Milo and Meg laughed together.

"Honestly! You two," Mom said, shaking her head. "If you would only be a little nicer to each other…"

**5**

The next day at school Milo found himself watching everyone more closely. He paid extra attention when Clarence was absent-mindedly doodling in Science class.

No, he thought. Sure, Clarence doodles, but how are we going to find the person who draws Icarus? How do we even start?

Meg was taking a Digital Art class. A few of her classmates drew their pictures by hand before transferring them into the computer, but no one did any watercolor painting, and no one drew in the style of Icarus.

Milo and Meg met on the school's front steps at the end of the school day.

"Any breakthrough?" Milo asked.

"Of course not. It could be anyone. It's probably a grown-up. How are we even going to begin looking?"

"I don't know."

They began walking.

Milo and Meg had done this walk so many times they could probably walk home from school with their eyes closed. They knew every step, every turn of the walk, by feel.

"What are we even looking for?" Meg asked.

"What do you mean? We're looking for an artist who draws these creatures."

"But, I mean…" Meg thought for a moment. "This person could be anywhere, right. It doesn't have to be someone here in August."

"So…" Milo took a moment to collect his thoughts. "So, are you saying someone might be drawing this somewhere else, but somehow we're living it here in August?"

"I don't know," Meg said. "I don't know what I'm saying."

"At least you admit you don't know what you're saying," Milo said from the corner of his mouth.

Meg smacked Milo's shoulder with her hand.

"Face it," Milo kept on. "You're absolutely no help at all."

"I'm no help? You're hopeless," Meg said laughing.

"Hi Milo. Hi Meg. We're going to have to start dinner without Mom tonight. That big new client of hers is keeping her at work late."

Dad wiped his hands on his apron and smiled at Milo and Meg.

"Whu'd you fix?" Milo asked.

"I'm trying a new lemon rice salmon. It's an experiment. Go easy on me if you don't like it."

Milo and Meg had long ago agreed that their dad was the World Champion Dork, but they had to admit that he was a darn good cook.

As the three of them sat down to test Dad's experiment, Meg decided to bring up some of the questions she had.

"Dad, who do you know of, in this city, who's an artist?"

"An Artist? What, you mean like oil painting?"

"No, watercolor. Pencil drawings."

"Are you thinking of taking lessons?"

Meg glanced quickly over at Milo.

"Um, sure, we both are, me and Milo."

"Really! Milo, your sister's speaking for you."

"No, she's right," Milo said. "I want to start drawing. I want to take classes."

"What about at school? Don't you have an art teacher? We have a good one at August High. Chuck Brown. Oh, there's your mother."

The familiar lights of Mom's car moved across the living room window and shut off quickly, in a scene they had been through hundreds times over the years.

A moment later Mom came in the door, tossed her work bag off her shoulder onto the couch, and gave everyone a slightly tired smile.

"My Sweeties," she said, hugging Meg from behind and kissing her on the cheek. Milo squirmed as she repeated the hug with him. "Honey, what is this? Salmon? Lemon? This looks delicious!"

"It's new. I'm experimenting."

"Kids, how is it?"

Meg smiled and looked at Milo. "Well, I don't want this to go to Dad's head," she said, "but, yeah, you know, it's...it's alright."

Mom turned to Dad. "Honey, coming from your daughter Meg, that is an amazing compliment." She turned back to Meg. "Give me just a minute and I'll come join you all." And she went down the hallway.

"So, what were we talking about? Oh yes, art teachers," Dad said.

"Well..." Milo glanced at Meg. "School has an art class, but it's so focused on computer art. We're interested in something a little different. We want to meet some of the best drawing teachers in town, just to, you know, meet them and, just, just, um, meet them."

"Meg, you feel the same way?"

Before she could answer, Mom returned to the table and sat down. She fussed for a minute over her plate.

"This already smells amazing, before I've even had a bite."

She scooped some rice onto her plate, then used the spatula to lift a piece of the salmon with a lemon wedge cooked onto it.

"Mm, I'm interrupting whatever you were talking about."

"Milo and I want to start taking some art lessons, drawing, watercolor. We want to meet some art teachers here in town."

"Art teachers!" Mom said. She took a bite and chewed slowly. "Honey! This is delicious! You've outdone yourself."

"Thanks," Dad said.

"Art classes," Mom said, chewing on a second bite. "Mm! Can't, can't you take art at school?"

"Sure," said Milo, "but we're looking for real professionals."

"Hm." Mom thought for a moment. "You both want this?"

Milo and Meg nodded their heads in agreement.

"Well, I think it's great that the two of you want something together. I'm okay with this, mostly because of that. I love that you two both have something you want together." She turned to Dad and waved her fork. "What do you think, Honey?"

"It seems like they should be able to get what they need at school, but if they want to meet other art teachers, I guess there's no harm in just going out and meeting people."

"Okay, sure," Mom said. "Alright, make a list of people around town, and we'll figure out how to go meet them."

"Cool," Milo said.

"Thanks," said Meg.

"It's about time you two found something to bond over a little bit."

6

The next day after school Milo and Meg stopped on the hill where the two trees stood next to each other.

They paused for a moment, then Milo squeezed between the trees and was gone.

Meg followed.

As they adjusted to being back in Icarus, they realized something was different. It was quiet.

Where was the usual danger and panic?

A Gort flew overhead, but it seemed to be flying more peacefully than normal; none of the aggressive attacking behavior that they had become used to.

"Ho! Ho! Milo and Meg!" It was Nanette's voice, shouting happily from the door of her hut across the field.

"Let's go," Milo said, and together they ran across the field.

As they came close to Nanette's hut they suddenly stopped running. Happy smiles spread across their faces.

"Wolf!" Meg shouted. "You're back!"

They all shared a few hugs.

Wolf was Nanette's son, grown up, like an older teenager, although sometimes he seemed younger, and occasionally he seemed a little bit older. It was hard to keep track, as his look sometimes changed subtly, even as they looked at him.

"It was the strangest thing," Nanette said. "This mornin' I was just wakin' up and I heard him snoring like a lumberjack sawing wood. There he was!"

"Where were you?" Milo asked.

"Nowhere," said Wolf.

"He has no memory of being gone," Nanette said.

Milo and Meg looked at Wolf curiously.

"What's your last memory?" Meg asked.

"I just remember being here, talking to the two of you. Then you left, to go back to the solid world..." He paused for a minute. "Later that night, though, as I was falling asleep, I had a strange sensation."

Nanette came over from the stove. "Strange sensation," she said. "Wolfy, what was this here strange sensation yer speaking of?"

"I was going away."

Milo, Meg, and Nanette held their breath.

"You didn't mention none of this 'goin' away' bizniss before," Nanette said, sounding slightly worried.

"My feet were going. Even the bed I was sleeping in was going. Then more of me was going. It was almost like I was falling asleep, except…"

"Exceptin' what, Wolfy?"

"…Except..I wasn't going to sleep at all. I was wide awake I was just disappearing…and then…then…I was…asleep, I guess. Then here I was this morning."

A long silence passed.

"Erased!" shouted Nanette. "You was erased! And then here you are redrawn!"

Milo and Meg looked blankly at each other.

Nanette turned to them. "You have to find him. The Artist. You have to let him know we're here. We're real. We're as real as he is. We think and feel. He can't just erase us. And…"

"And what, Nanette?" Meg had turned her head slightly sideways.

"And, the others."

"Others?"

"Wolfy and I aren't alone. Our friends. The others. Where are they? There used to be a whole village here. Where are they?"

"A whole village..." Milo's eyes were wide with surprise and worry.

Nanette put a pot of water on the stove. She stared down into the water for a moment.

"I have a sister," she said. "Janice." She looked over at Wolf. "Wolfy...do you remember Auntie Janice?"

Wolf shook his head. He was trying to look back into his past. "I don't remember," he said.

Milo looked over at Meg. "We have to go out and explore."

Meg nodded. She turned to Nanette. "We're going to look for the Artist, but we don't exactly know what we're looking for. Can – can we just go out exploring? I don't even know exactly what we expect to find..."

"Of course you'll go explore," Nanette said. "Do whatever you can. Just be careful about them Gorts. They seem calm and peaceful this morning, but that could turn on a dime. Thems is rash, turn-on-a-dime foul smellin' evil creatures, if you ask me."

7

Milo and Meg stood on the freshly drawn grass outside Nanette's hut. They gazed across the long valley that stretched out in front of them, the mountains sloping up on each side, and the thick forest of trees at the far end of the valley.

Most of the trees and mountain sides were painted with watercolors, but a few small areas were still black and white, pencil drawings, like Milo and Meg themselves, seemingly unfinished, but still here. They walked on the grass as if it were a solid world.

Behind them Nanette and Wolf stood together in the doorway of the hut, waving goodbye.

Meg waved back, and together Milo and Meg began walking.

"Be careful," Nanette shouted. "If you smell anything wretched and foul, it's one of them forsaken Gorts. Take cover."

"We'll be careful," Meg said. Then, quietly, to Milo she said, "Where are the Gorts, anyway? Why don't we see any?"

"Good question," Milo said.

"That's all you have to say? 'Good question'?"

"Hey, what else do you want?"

"Oh, I don't know, maybe some kind of actual answer?"

They tried to walk as quietly as possible, but the steady 'scrunch scrunch' of their feet on the ground sounded louder than it ever had before.

This was different from their walks home from school, where they knew every detail without having to look. Everything here was new, and…oddly…changing.

"Was that tree there before?" Meg asked, pointing at a medium-height scraggly, leafy tree.

Milo stopped and looked at it. Then he turned behind him and gasped. Meg turned to see what had made him gasp, but all she saw was the valley they had been walking through. "What is it?" she asked.

Milo blinked and rubbed his eyes.

"It was the weirdest thing." He blinked a couple more times and shook his head. "When I first turned around, nothing was there."

"Nothing?"

"Blank, like…like it was blank white paper. But then suddenly it was all there again."

Meg looked back at the valley behind them. It was beautiful. The greens of the trees were deep greens. There were yellows and oranges that seemed to jump off the page. She had to remind herself that this was not a normal world, that this beauty – this beauty that she was walking through, was a drawing, and an unfinished watercolor painting.

She turned back to her brother and said, "This is just a little bit strange."

"You think?"

"Yeah, I think."

"Wait a minute. What…" Milo was looking intently at something near the ground.

"Hm?" Meg followed his gaze. "What the –"

Together they bent down close to the ground. There, next to a tree root, barely readable, almost on the ground, but actually floating just above the ground, were letters, letters that spelled the word, "Phoebe."

"Milo! Meg! Are you two ready to go?"

"A minute, Mom. Almost." Meg shook her head impatiently at the drawing Milo held. "I mean, it has the same kind of style, I guess, but it's obviously not the same artist. And it's signed FJ27. Whoever FJ27 is, it sure isn't "Phoebe"

"No, you're right," Milo said, closing the book. "Who the heck is Phoebe? There's no Phoebe in this whole town."

"Milo! Meg!"

"Coming!"

They grudgingly stopped what they were doing and headed downstairs.

The car ride to the party was maddening. Dad drove, while Mom kept going on and on about Ramsey Fisher. Ramsey Fisher did this. Ramsey Fisher did that.

"Mom, why do we have to go to this party?" Milo moaned.

"Oh, come on. There will be other kids there, maybe even someone you know from school."

"Oh my god, it's all going to be the rich kids who don't like us."

"Well, Honey." Mom twisted around from the passenger seat to look at Milo. "You could stand to be nicer to the ones you call 'the rich kids.' It never hurts to have rich friends in your corner."

Mom was dragging Milo and Meg along to Mr. Fisher's 60th birthday bash.

Fisher was an eccentric old billionaire, who insisted that party-goers bring their whole families. He loved kids, he always said, even though he had never had any of his own.

The gate to the mansion was standing wide open. Dad drove the car into the round-circle driveway and parked behind a brand new red sports car.

They stepped out of the car and closed the doors. Milo, Meg, Mom and Dad began walking toward the mansion. It was easily the biggest house Milo or Meg had ever seen in their lives.

"This dude lives here alone?" Meg asked.

"He has a few people who live here with him," Mom said. "Helpers, employees, but he treats them all exactly like family."

The sounds of an old peoples' party drifted out from the mansion. As they approached the door, it opened for them.

"Welcome," the butler said.

"Wolf!" mom shouted happily and gave the butler a hug.

Milo and Meg turned to each other, and their eyes met in quiet surprise. Milo put his hand over his mouth.

Meg put her finger to her lips to keep Milo quiet.

They entered the mansion and the butler led them through the grand main entrance hall to the back patio, where 30 or 40 people, wearing expensive clothes, mingled and chatted.

"Ah! Here you are!"

A 60-year old man, gray hair piled on his head like it was just dumped there, came toward the family with open arms.

"Ramsey!" Mom said, giving him a hug. "This is my husband."

"Pleasure to met you. I've heard so much."

"Hopefully all good things," Dad said dorkishly, shaking Mr. Fisher's hand.

"And these are my sweet children, Milo and Meg."

"Hello."

"Hi"

Milo and Meg took awkward turns shaking the billionaire's hand.

"What lovely kids. Wolf, let's get these kids whatever they want…Well, whatever you want as long as it's kid friendly." Fisher laughed proudly at his own joke. "Let's go say hello to everyone."

He turned toward the mingling crowd, and Mom and Dad followed him.

Milo and Meg stood still and tried to make sense of things.

The butler, acting a little bit too polite, walked up to them. "Would you like a soda?" he asked.

"Sure," Meg said. "Root beer."

"And for the gentleman?" the butler said, turning to Milo.

"Is your name actually Wolf?" Milo asked as casually as he could.

Meg nearly smacked him from behind with her fist.

"Indeed," the butler said, smiling. "Short for Wolfgang."

"Two root beers," Meg said.

The butler nodded. "I'll be back with them in a moment." Then he turned away.

As Milo predicted, there were a few kids they knew from school at the party, and, as Milo predicted, they were the snobby rich kids who didn't really like Milo and Meg.

Jeremy Prescott walked past and tried to pretend he didn't see them, but Meg decided to call him out.

"Hi Jeremy," she said, smiling sideways.

"Oh, hey," Jeremy said, pretending he was happy to see them. "Meg, Milo, I didn't know you were here."

"Uh huh." Meg just stared at him, smiling, letting him know he was busted.

"Well, hey, good to see you," Jeremy said. He waved half-heartedly, and walked away awkwardly.

Milo and Meg laughed together

Wolf came back with the two root beers.

"Your beverages," he said.

"Thanks Wolf," Milo said. "Hey Wolf, is it bad manners to ask your last name?"

"Indeed no, I do not consider it bad manners. My last name is Cunningham. Why, if I may ask, are you so curious about my name?"

Milo glanced over at Meg, and said, unconvincingly, "Oh, nothing, no, no reason. I'm just, uh, we're just, um, collecting people's names."

"Indeed," Wolf said. He bowed slightly to Milo and Meg, and said, "If you'll excuse me," before turning to the crowd.

Milo and Meg hardly participated in the party. They found a corner of the large patio partially hidden by leaves and branches and sat together.

"Does it mean anything, or are we crazy?" Meg asked

"His name is Wolfgang. It's a perfectly normal name for such a butler-y person. It probably doesn't mean anything."

"So...the answer is, we're crazy?"

"No," Milo said. "Just you. I never said I was crazy."

Meg smiled at her brother and looked out at the sprawling mansion. "I don't know. These rich people. They always have secrets, you know. You can never believe them."

"What do you mean?" Milo asked.

"People like this are always hiding something."

"What are you suggesting?"

Meg didn't answer right away.

Finally, Milo tried to answer his own question. "Should we look around the house?"

"Are you suggesting we go snooping?" Meg asked.

"Well…." Milo shrugged. He twisted his face, then said, "Yeah…I think we should snoop around a little."

Meg nodded.

Together they walked casually through the mingling crowd.

"Kids!" Mom shouted. "Are you enjoying the party?"

"More than I could have ever imagined," Meg answered sarcastically.

They kept walking toward the house, trying their best to act casual.

They walked through the open double glass doors and found themselves watching a small kitchen staff of five working busily.

They moved into a large open living room.

To the right was a stairway that curved up along the wall.

This stairway struck both Milo and Meg as interesting.

They looked around.

No one else was in the room. No one was paying any attention to them.

They went to the stairway and quickly went up.

At the top they found a hallway with several doors on each side. All the doors were closed.

"What do you think?" Milo asked. "You think these doors have alarms?"

"Yes," Meg said, matter-of-factly. "I think if we try to open one, we would both be completely and totally busted."

They shared a disappointed sigh.

Slowly they went back down the stairs.

"How can we find out more about this place?" Milo asked.

Meg's face lit up with a smile. "I know exactly what we can do," she said.

"What?"

"Milo! It's obvious. Think. Where are we?"

"At Ramey Fisher's house," he answered.

"Exactly!"

"Oh…so…you think we should start hanging out with Mom and Dad's friends and act like we want to be here?"

"Good boy, Milo," Meg said teasingly. "You're getting smarter."

"Oh, you kids," Mom said from the front seat, as Dad drove them home. "I'm so glad you found a way to enjoy the party. I was worried at first. Mr. Fisher took quite a liking to the two of you."

"Yeah? You think so?" Meg asked.

"Absolutely, Meg. He thought you were the funniest, smartest girl in the world. And, Milo, what a charmer you can be when you try."

"Thanks, Mom."

Dad drove the car in silence for a minute.

"Mm, well," Mom muttered to no one and everyone. "What time is it, anyway?"

9

The next morning was Saturday, and Milo and Meg had work to do.

They had eaten a quick breakfast and headed out of the house, up the hill to the twin trees.

They hardly hesitated anymore, before squeezing between the trees and entering Icarus.

Instantly a barrage of incoming spears and arrows sent Milo and Meg diving into thick tree cover.

"The gawd fersakin' Gorts are rampaging!"

It was Nannette's unmistakable voice.

"Show your faces, you whiney, ugly, gawd-fersaken creatures!"

Nanette was aiming an old cross bow into the sky. She was yelling in a way Milo and Meg and not seen before. She seemed more wild than usual, as if something had snapped in her.

"Come on, you dirty flying rodents! What are you, afraid to show your faces? Just try it, and you'll git what's comin' to yu!"

Milo and Meg gave each other wide eyed looks of worry.

"Nanette!" Meg yelled.

"Yu DEVIL creatures! Come on, where are yu?"

Then that newly unmistakable sound of an incoming barrage of projectiles whistled in the air. Milo and Meg ducked at the base of a tree, covering their heads.

Then the thwack thwack thwack of several deadly sharp points stabbing into the ground one after the other in quick succession.

"Is that all you got?" Nanette spat out, defiantly standing, exposed, but unhurt. "Next time you send another cowardly round o' these spears, they're all comin' back at you! Yeah, you better watch out. These are comin' BACK!"

"Nanette!" This time it was Milo trying to get her attention.

"Yeah! Whaddyu want?"

"You need to protect yourself. Get down!"

"It's too darn late for that," Nanette spat out. "They dun already burned down the hut and kidnapped Wolf! Two bit thieves and kidnappers is what they are! You cowards! Yer afraid tu show yer faces!"

"Nanette!" Meg yelled. "Let's find someplace safe, so we can talk. Come on."

Meg stood and was trying to pull Nanette by the hand deeper into the forest.

"These disfigured, deformed creatures are gonna regret the day they were drawn!"

"Nanette!"

Milo had joined Meg in trying to lead Nanette away

Grudgingly, an exhausted and dejected Nanette turned and followed them into the thick undergrowth.

"Evil creatures!" Nanette yelled, as they walked.

Eventually they had walked far enough, and entered a thick enough section of forest, that they felt safe slowing down. Meg sat on a log. Milo leaned his back against a tree trunk. Nanette turned randomly, still lost in whatever trauma had happened earlier.

Meg spoke first, placing a calm hand on Nanette's flailing arm. "Nanette, are you okay?"

"Heck no, I'm not okay," she snapped.

"What happened? What happened to your hut? Where's Wolf?"

"Them Gorts are on a rampage. Who even knows why? What do you want? WHAT DO YOU WANT?" she yelled up into the air.

"Sh! Nanette!" Milo whispered urgently. "Let's stay as quiet as we can. I don't know exactly what's going on, but I think it's important that we stay as quiet as possible."

Nanette disgustedly threw a stick into the grass.

The three of them took a breath.

"Okay," Meg said, "what's going on?"

"They attacked for no reason." Nanette was still very agitated. "The hut started burning, so we ran out. Then one of them gawd fersaken creatures grabbed Wolf in its claws and flew off with him.

Neither Milo or Meg knew what to say.

They sat silently.

Eventually Milo found the courage to speak.

"We have to go find him."

"What we have to do is kill all them creatures," Nanette said.

Meg looked over at Nanette.

"Whatever plan we go with, we have to make sure it doesn't get US killed."

"You won't be killed," Nanette scoffed. "You're solids. Look at you. Nothing will happen to you."

"We don't know that," Meg said, looking down at herself. "We don't know what happens to us here. Anything could happen. We have to be careful."

Milo cleared his throat. "We have to be sneaky and stealthy. Meg is right, we don't know what can and can't happen to us here, so we have to assume we could be hurt, injured, even killed. We have to find their base. We have to get there without them knowing we're there. We have to be absolutely silent. We have to travel under the cover of the forest. We have to be invisible. Otherwise we know what they'll do."

Meg, Nanette, and Milo all looked at each other.

Nanette looked down at the ground.

"Can you do it, Nanette?" Meg asked quietly. "Can you travel with us quietly? No outbursts?"

Nanette did not answer right away.

She looked up at Meg.

"I know the way," she said calmly. "It will be hard to stay quiet, but I can do it."

"Okay," Milo said.

Together the three of them stood up. Milo brushed some dirt off his pant leg, and turned his head, as if stretching out a kink in his neck.

Nanette quietly began walking.

Milo and Meg followed her.

Nanette led them through the thick forest. Trees towered above them blocking out the sunlight, casting suspicious shadows as they walked.

Progress was slow. They climbed over large fallen tree trunks, stepped in hidden sinkholes, bumped up against trees they did not even see until they suddenly appeared in front of them.

They picked their way through the forest this way, no one saying anything, for what seemed like more than an hour.

Then Milo and Meg seemed to have lost Nanette.

She was ahead of them but not that far ahead. One moment they were following her. The next moment she was not there.

All was quiet.

Meg looked left and right but saw nothing.

Milo held himself totally still, listening, scanning his ears around the surrounding forest, listening for any recognizable sound.

Then they heard Nanette's whisper a few feet away.

"Hey!"

Milo moved toward the sound. Meg moved behind her brother.

Nanette was curled up and hunched over behind a large bush.

"Sh!" she whispered.

Milo crawled close to Nanette and hid behind the bush next to her. Meg crawled to the other side of Nanette.

"Look," Nanette whispered.

She held aside a branch and revealed what looked like a small village in the distance.

Gorts flew calmly from place to place in the village. Everything seemed too calm. Gort families went about their business. Gort children ran and flew and played with a lighthearted, carefree attitude.

It all looked too peaceful.

"He's in there somewhere," Nanette whispered.

She looked over at Meg.

"What do we do now?" Meg asked.

"We sneak our way in," Nanette whispered back. "One of us does, anyways."

Milo turned from the open branches. "What happens if they hear us?" he whispered.

Nanette exhaled. "Everything might look peaceful right now. Don't be fooled. These are foul, sick creatures. If they find us here, there's no telling what they'll do to us."

"What are they doing to Wolf?" Meg asked.

"Torture!" Nanette spat back. "They probably have him strung up by his hands and feet."

"Why?" Milo seemed genuinely shocked.

"They don't have a reason. They don't need reasons," Nanette said. Then she reached into a deep hidden pocket of her garment. She pulled out a shirt with stitching on it. "Put this on," Nanette said, handing the shirt to Milo.

Milo took the shirt and held it out in front of him. "Why? What's it for?"

"It's what my grandfather called a 'Shadow shirt.'"

"What does it do?"

"It hasn't been worn since my grandfather wore it. There's an old legend about that shirt, that the wearer can't be seen."

"But..." Milo held the shirt up against his torso. "But, you don't know if it's true?"

"No one's put it on. We treat the shadow shirt with too much respect. We grow up being told never wear it unless you have no other choice."

Milo looked back out at the distant village. He looked at Nanette. Slowly, hesitantly, he slipped the shirt over his head. Half-way on, he slipped his arms through the arm holes, and pulled it down around his waist.

"That's a fine looking shirt, young man," Nanette said.

"It doesn't work," said Meg. "I can still see him."

"Enemies," spat Nanette. "You are only invisible from your enemies."

Milo and Meg looked at each other with concern.

"What now?" Milo asked.

"Well..." Nanette looked out through the bushes. "Now you sneak on over and look for my Wolfy."

Milo felt a calm come over him, as he stood and faced the village. After a moment he pushed the branches aside and stepped forward.

He moved into a clearing. If the Gorts were going to come after him, now would be their moment.

No Gort came.

Milo took a step forward, and then another step.

He was walking toward the village. He continued across the clearing and finally came to the first hut at the edge of the village.

Now, he thought to himself, I just have to figure which hut Wolf is in. He walked among the huts quietly. Gorts flew and walked about their business, and none paid any attention to Milo.

He listened as he passed each hut. He strained to hear whatever sounds he could, listening for any sign of someone in distress.

Each hut he came to, he stopped and listened for any sounds from inside. Most were silent inside. Others gave off the sound of peacefulness, of a Gort family living inside.

He moved quietly from one hut to the next. This went on for what seemed like ages, as he moved from hut to hut.

His disappointment became consistent. Each new hut was frustrating. Then he was tempted to get lazy.

He stepped up to another hut, now expecting the disappointing silence again.

Then...something made him stop.

He wasn't sure what he was hearing at first.

Someone sounded angry. Maybe it was just an argument, he thought. These Gort families can't all be perfectly happy.

He struggled to hear what was being said inside. He put his ear to the outer wall of the hut, closed his eyes, and strained to hear.

It was yelling. He couldn't make out the words.

Then he heard Wolf's voice.

Was it? Was that?...Was that Wolf?

He kept his eyes closed and poured all concentration into listening.

Yes...yes, that has to be Wolf's voice.

Milo's heart began thumping in his chest, as adrenaline surged into him.

He felt scared and brave, and full of fear, and full of determination, all at the same time.

Now what? Milo thought to himself. With the shadow shirt they can't see me, but they would see a door open. How do I...

Slowly, carefully, Milo began a quiet slow walk all the way around the hut. He was looking, just looking, for anything, a weak spot, something missing, anything to grab his attention.

Then he came to an open window.

He peeked his eyes around the corner of the window frame.

Just as Nanette had predicted, Wolf was tied by his hands and feet. He was stretched out on a bed, unable to move. The ropes were tied to each of his hands and feet, pulling them in four different directions.

"You'll pay the price for your evil," a voice shouted.

Then Milo saw him, an old angry Gort, scaly, breathing fire-smelling breath, and standing at the foot of the bed Wolf was strapped to.

"My family has done nothing," Wolf protested.

"Your family, your great great great grandfather burned this village many many years ago."

"My g...my great great great grandfather! I never even knew my great great grandfather! I never knew him!"

"Vengeance knows no generations," shouted the Gort.

Milo wondered what his next move could possibly be. He wished Meg were with him. Meg always had good ideas.

Milo slumped down below the window and leaned his back against the wall of the hut.

He waited there. He was not sure what he was waiting for. He just waited for something to inspire him.

He listened…

Silence.

Slowly, carefully, Milo stood up and looked through the window. Wolf was there, still stretched out and tied, but no one else was in the room.

As quietly as he could, Milo climbed in the open window. He was careful not to make any noise. Wearing the shadow shirt might make him invisible, he thought, but it does not make him silent. If they heard him they would surely attack him.

Milo delicately let himself down from the window ledge. He half expected Wolf to turn and see him, but Wolf saw nothing and heard nothing.

Milo stood looking at Wolf. Wolf's eyes were open, looking straight up toward the ceiling.

Why doesn't Wolf see me, Milo thought.

Then the door to the room burst open, and the old scaly Gort came into the room.

Milo froze.

"We have decided to let you drink water," the Gort spat out, carrying a small bottle. "If you ask me, we should let you suffer, but I have been over-ruled."

Then the Gort stopped, lifted his head, and looked around the room.

Again, Milo's heart thumped heavily inside his chest.

The Gort's searching eyes looked right past Milo.

The Gort sniffed the air.

He sniffed a second time.

"What is that?" The Gort asked.

"Hm?" Wolf was confused by the question.

"That smell! What is that smell?"

Milo's heart nearly jumped out of his chest.

The Gort threw down his water bottle and quickly left the room.

Milo knew he had to act quickly.

He jumped to the side of Wolf. He tore at the knot in the rope near Wolf's left hand.

Wolf did not know what was happening.

Suddenly his left hand was free. He did not know why. Then his right hand was free. His left foot. His right foot.

"Out the window!" Milo whispered.

"Who's here?" asked Wolf.

"Out the window! Now!"

"Milo!" Wolf had recognized the voice.

"Go! Jump!"

Wolf hurried to the window. He didn't think. He just moved. He stuck a leg over the ledge and slipped down to the ground below.

Milo followed.

He dropped to the ground just as the door opened and three Gorts entered the room.

They breathed angry breath as they discovered the straps empty, where Wolf had been just moments before.

Outside, Milo leaned over Wolf, covering him as completely as he could. He did not know if the shadow shirt would work this way, covering two people, but he had to try.

The Gorts came to the window and looked out.

Milo gently covered Wolf's mouth with his hand, letting Wolf know to be as quiet as possible.

The Gorts saw nothing.

Nasty smelling breath poured angrily from their nostrils.

Together the three Gorts turned to leave the room.

Now Milo felt stuck. He was not sure what to do.

"We have a problem," Milo said.

"We..." Wolf repeated. "I think you mean I have a problem."

"I'm wearing your mother's shadow shirt. It makes me invisible. It seems to make you invisible when I cover you. But I don't know how we get out of here without one of us being seen."

The words were barely out of his mouth when a loud siren went off across the village. It was ear-piercing, a high pitched whining siren that caused Milo and Wolf to cover their ears in agony.

Gorts scurried through the town, everyone suddenly desperate to get home. Within moments the entire village seemed eerily empty and quiet.

Milo brought his head up as one last straggler was closing the door of his hut, followed by the finality of a lock-bolt being locked from inside the door.

Milo looked to his left. He looked to his right. The village was still, silent, eerie.

"Okay," Milo began...but he had nothing else to say.

"I know how we can do this," Wolf whispered.

"How?"

"We stay together. You keep me covered. We move as one, but we have to stay off the roads. We move from hut to hut, yard to yard, slowly, silently. It's the only way."

Milo looked out from the corner of the hut they had escaped from. "Which way do we go?" he asked.

"This way," Wolf said, pointing to the next hut closest to them.

"Okay."

Together Milo and Wolf crawled, Milo holding the ghost shirt over Wolf the best he could.

They quickly crawled across the patch of open grass to the corner of the next hut.

Success!

They leaned their backs against the wall of the hut.

"How far do we have to go?" Milo asked.

Wolf did not answer. He gave Milo a look.

Hut by hut, yard by yard, Milo and Wolf slowly made their way through the village. They crawled. They walked. They half-ran, staying as silent as they could.

For most of their silent journey they saw no one, no Gorts. The further they traveled through the town, the more confident they felt. They moved faster.

Maybe they had become too confident, too casual, too certain they had already escaped the danger.

They were near the edge of the village. Milo looked out around the corner of the last hut and saw the empty field that led back to Nanette and Meg's hiding place. He put his hand above his eyes in order to focus his vision.

He stood all the way up

"There!" shouted a voice.

Milo turned.

Wolf was uncovered.

The Gorts had seen him and were flying rapidly toward them.

Milo dropped down over Wolf and smothered him with the shadow shirt.

"Move to a new spot!" Wolf whispered urgently.

Together they rolled to their left under a bush.

Everything became silent.

Slowly, carefully, a Gort foot stepped in the grass in front of them. The foot was inches away from Milo's nose. He could smell the unwashed foot.

The foot remained still, ominously standing, offering its silent but deadly smell, while Milo and Wolf did their best to hold their breath.

Eventually Milo had to let out a breath of air, trying his best to exhale without making a sound.

Then another Gort foot joined.

Quiet talking filtered down to Milo's ears, but he couldn't make out what they were saying.

Then one of the Gorts spoke louder.

"Scan the area!" it shouted. "He's hiding here somewhere."

Milo's heart jumped a beat.

Other Gorts, he knew, were flying above them, hovering, scanning and looking down over the whole area.

Wolf calmly twisted under Milo and whispered directly into Milo's ear.

"Simple," he said.

Milo looked at him with an expression that seemed to say, "Tell me more."

"We wait."

Afraid of making any extra noise, Milo simply squinted at Wolf.

"We wait till dark. We wait them out."

Milo nodded. Then worry settled on him. Then he exhaled, and settled in for a long wait.

10

Nanette and Meg, still in their hiding place among the bushes, saw the Gorts flying over the edge of the village.

Nanette was smiling.

"You're not worried?" Meg asked.

"My boy Wolfy..." Nanette said, leaving the thought unfinished.

"You think he's safe?"

"Look at those dumb flying beasts," Nanette said. "They're looking for him. It's a beautiful sight. Ha ha! Oh, my boy Wolfy."

Meg allowed herself to smile faintly.

"How do they get out, though?" Meg asked. "Wherever they're hiding, the Gorts will see them if they move."

"My boy Wolfy is smarter than those foul-smelling creatures. He'll wait them out, even if it takes all night."

Milo opened his eyes with a start.

It was dark.

He had been asleep.

He turned his head. Wolf was sleeping quietly next to him.

Without moving, Milo tried to peek out through the leaves. He couldn't make anything out. He listened. All he heard was silence.

They were still there, though. He could feel them

Wolf sputtered and half woke up.

"Sh." Milo covered Wolf's mouth with his hand.

Wolf blinked and took a moment to collect himself.

They were both fully awake now.

Milo tried to guess how deep into the night it was. Time was a blur. It was dark, that's all he knew. The only thing Milo was sure of was that their moment was right now.

"Let's go," he whispered.

Wolf nodded.

Together, being extra careful to stay together in the shadow shirt, Wolf and Milo crawled out from under the bush they had been hiding under.

They moved slowly, making as little noise as they could.

They were in the open, exposed.

Milo carefully turned his head to look behind him.

He saw them, two sentinels standing in the grass. They did not see him.

Another Gort hovered in the air a short ways away. That one also seemed unaware of his presence.

Milo turned back and together he and Wolf crawled forward.

Their progress was agonizingly slow.

They were only half-way across the clearing when they both heard a noise.

They stopped. They looked back. They heard the sentinels talking, but could not make out what they were saying.

The two sentinels walked away, replaced by two new ones.

"Just changing the watch," Wolf whispered.

They stayed still for what felt like five more minutes.

All was quiet again.

"Okay," Wolf finally said.

They resumed their agonizingly slow progress.

Finally they reached the edge of the clearing.

They crawled under a bizarrely arched bush and found Nanette and Meg sleeping.

Meg rested her head on Nanette's stomach, rising and falling ever so slightly as Nanette breathed.

Milo finally took the shadow shirt off, and whispered into his sister's ear.

"Meg!"

"MM!" Meg opened her eyes with a shock.

"Sh."

"Milo!"

"Sh."

Nanette opened her eyes. "Wolfy!" she whispered happily.

"Sh!" This time it was Meg worried about the noise they were suddenly making.

Nanette and Wolf hugged each other, and everyone took a deep breath.

"Well done," Nanette whispered. "Now let's get the heck out of here."

"Do you know our way out?" Milo asked.

"Trust us," Wolf said. "We'll get you out."

It was too dark to see, but Wolf stepped into the thickly forested woods, and moved forward as if he could see clearly. Meg fell in behind him and Milo behind her. Nanette waited to bring up the rear.

As Wolf bounded his way over fallen tree trunks, Nanette called to Wolf to slow down several times.

After an hour of this difficult dark travel Wolf finally stopped.

"Here," he said. "This is where you can return to your solid world."

Meg looked around in the dark. She struggled to make out where they were, but eventually she began to recognize the area.

"What about you two?" she asked, looking from Wolf to Nanette. "How will you stay safe?"

Neither answered at first.

"Find the Artist," Nanette finally said. "Find the one who draws us. Tell him we need his help."

Milo and Meg looked to each other, and then back to Nanette. "He...might be a 'her," Meg said. "The Artist...might be a woman."

Nanette stared intently at Meg. "I'm sure The Artist is a 'he'."

An awkward pause passed and then they turned.

They both saw it and both stopped moving for just a moment. There it was again. This time it was written in mid-air between two trees. It was the name they had seen once before; "Phoebe."

They gazed at it for a moment before shaking their focus back to Nanette and Wolf.

They turned to the two trees, and slowly, carefully, stepped back into their normal world.

Once again they were standing on the hill in the city of August.

It was sunny.

They both had to rub their eyes against the shock of going from dead-of-night to bright Saturday morning. They were back in the place - and the time - they had left. It had seemed like days ago, but as always, no time had passed.

I'll never get used to this," Meg said.

"I know," said Milo. "How long were we in there?"

They walked down the hill to the street.

They walked home silently. They felt little need to talk to each other. All they could do was walk.

## Part Three

## 11

"Well, THERE you two are! Where in the world are you going this early on a Saturday? Come on, let's get ready. The Ambersons will lose patience."

Milo and Meg's mom pulled a jacket out of the hall closet impatiently.

Milo looked at Meg with a confused, twisted face.

"Where are we going, Mom?" Meg asked

"The Ambersons, of course."

"Who are the Ambersons?"

"The husband and wife Art-teaching team I told you about...Didn't I tell you? Well, maybe I forgot. Anyway, get yourselves ready. You'll love 'em."

Meg gave Milo a defeated expression, and they shrugged at each other. Milo turned to Mom.

"I think, uh, I think we're ready, I guess."

Meg looked awkwardly down at her feet. "Do we...have to go?"

Mom turned sternly to Meg. "Now look. You two brought this up. You sounded so sure that this was what you wanted. You two share so little with each other. Sometimes I wonder if you're really even brother and sister. You wanted this. Now, I think it's a perfect thing to follow up on."

"Since when do we not share anything with each other?" Meg complained. "Of course we share stuff. It's you and Dad I'm worried about. I'm beginning to wonder if you're really our parents. It's like we came from different families and were accidentally switched at birth by evil nurses!"

Milo's eyes widened in Meg's direction. He gave her a look that said calm down a little. Meg caught the look, and knew she'd stepped over a line.

"...That was uncalled-for," Mom said. "Maybe we should cancel this meet-up. Maybe I should ground you for being so mouthy!"

"Sorry, Mom. Sorry." Meg looked down at her feet, but was secretly rolling her eyes at the ridiculousness of the moment.

"Look me in the eye, and tell me you're sorry," Mom said.

Meg took a breath, rolled her eyes one last time, and looked up at her mom as innocently as she could.

"I'm sorry, Mom. Maybe I'm being a little too crabby."

Mom did not say anything for a minute. She looked at her daughter, feeling slightly hurt. Finally she sighed and said, "Thank you for apologizing. Honestly, being your mother can be challenging at times, with that mouth you have on you. Now, hurry up. Let's get going."

She moved to the door, and Milo reluctantly followed. He was smiling a sly smile at Meg, as she covered her mouth with her hand to hide the fit of sarcastic giggles that had suddenly come over her.

The car ride was awkward in all the normal awkward ways.

Milo escaped most of the awkwardness by beating Meg into the back seat.

Meg gave him a glare as she reached for the front door and climbed in next to Mom.

"How'd you do on that history test?" Mom asked Meg as she turned the wheel and drove down the street.

"Good," Meg said, matter-of-factly.

Mom looked over at her. "That's all? 'Good'? You have nothing more to tell your mom?"

"Well," Meg searched her brain for something to say that would not get her into trouble. "I had to figure out the difference between the Articles of Confederation and the Constitutional Convention. That was kinda if-y, but I managed to get it right in the end."

"Very good, then, " Mom said. "I'm proud of you for starting to pay attention in class."

Meg decided to let the back-handed compliment go, and turned toward the car window. she hoped her mom would quit making her talk, and buried her attention in the same passing trees and houses that she had looked at a million times before.

The Ambersons instantly rubbed Milo and Meg the wrong way.

"Tell me what you dream about," Marcia Amberson said, as she led them through the living room into a large art studio in the next room.

Neither Milo or Meg answered at first.

Ned Amberson was standing on the third rung of a ladder dabbing a brush on a giant canvas. He turned as they entered the room. "Hello!" he said enthusiastically. "Forgive me for not shaking hands. I'm covered in paint."

It was true. Ned wore white coveralls that were hardly white anymore. Red, yellow, green and blue oil splotches gave his coveralls more of a tie-dyed look. More paint covered parts of his hands and even his left cheek.

The giant canvas covered most of the wall. Is was colorful but random. Milo and Meg shared a look that confirmed their worst fear; this was not what they were looking for. They couldn't explain to their mom, at this point, that they were less interested in oil painting than in searching the town of August for a mysterious pencil and watercolor artist who goes by 'Phoebe.'

"So, you didn't answer my question," Marcia said, as Ned made his way carefully down the ladder.

"Kids?" Mom gave Milo and Meg an impatient look.

"Hm? You want to know what we - " Meg searched her brain for the rest of the question.

"What you dream about," repeated Marcia.

Meg turned to Milo.

They shared another unspoken thought; how the heck can we get out of here without making everyone mad at us?

"I mostly dream of burying Milo alive," Meg said.

Milo snickered silently at the joke, but Meg instantly regretted saying it, as the three adults turned to her sternly.

Marcia Amberson cleared her throat. "Art," she began, "is our subconscious mind screaming to speak freely. Art is in all of us. All we have to do is let go of our little hang-ups, let go of the daily concerns that trap us in this temporal world. Art aches for release." She reached over to touch her husband's elbow. "Ned and I are living out a passion for creative expression, and we have an equal passion for passing on this freedom to our students."

Meg tried to settle down the battle going on in her head; don't crack up! Don't crack up! Look serious. Nod your head. Make everyone think you're listening. Don't crack up! Don't crack up! DON'T Cra - oh HELP!

She lost the battle.

Milo and Meg were laughing uncontrollably as Mom pulled them by the elbows back through the Ambersons living room, out their front door, and down the steps to the driveway.

Together, they laughed on top of each other as they climbed into the back seat of the car, Meg was barely able to scoot to the opposite side before the out-of-control giggling Milo dropped on top of her.

Mom started the car angrily and backed onto the street.

The angry, embarrassed silence from mom was thick in the car, but Milo and Meg continued to share the giggle fit for blocks before Mom finally spoke.

"I hope you two are happy!" she barked, turning left onto Silver Avenue.

"Oh, we are," Milo snickered.

Nothing else was said the rest of the way home.

Meg loved her brother in that moment. No one else in this world made sense to her.

12

Milo lay flat on his back staring up at the ceiling of his bedroom. "We haven't solved anything," he said, "and now we're grounded."

Meg was also lying on her back, on the floor next to Milo's bed, where she couldn't see him.

She tossed a tennis ball straight up toward the ceiling. It slowed, just barely stopping before hitting the ceiling, then curved over the bed and dropped into Milo's open hand.

"We have to find 'Phoebe,'" he said tossing the ball back up toward the ceiling.

Meg opened her hand and casually caught the tennis ball as it dropped to her.

"I'm out of ideas," she said.

She tossed the ball back up.

Milo didn't say anything this time, silently agreeing with her, but refusing to accept defeat.

He tossed the ball back up. Meg caught it again.

They tossed the tennis ball back and forth a few more times without talking.

Finally Meg said what she was thinking.

"Look," she said, "we have to keep looking. There's no time to lose. We have to do a search. We have to find every name in town that has anything to do with this 'Phoebe.'"

Milo sat up and scooted to the edge of the bed. He looked down at his sister lying flat on her back on the floor. He carefully stepped over her and sat on the half-broken chair next to a small desk. He opened the laptop.

Milo typed 'Phoebe' and waited for the results.

"It's just a bunch of people named 'Phoebe,'" Milo said. We need a last name."

Meg tossed the tennis ball but didn't say anything.

Milo shook his head at the computer screen.

Their mutual silent frustration was broken by Dad knocking on the door.

"Milo? Meg?"

Milo stood up and opened the door.

"Alright if I come in?" Dad asked.

"Sure." Milo stepped aside, carefully avoid his sister. Meg finally sat up as Dad walked in the room.

"Look," he said, doing his best impression of a dorky but sensitive parent. "I know things haven't been perfect in this family recently."

Milo and Meg didn't respond, at least not to their dad. The quick look they gave each other, though, said all they needed to say.

"You're going to stay grounded for the rest of the weekend, but we thought we'd let you come with us to have lunch at Mr. Ramseys' house. It's sort of a, you know…" he struggled to find the right comparison.

"…Work release from prison?" Meg said.

Dad looked sideways. "Maybe," he said. "Anyway, let's get you two ready. We're about to go."

Milo and Meg snickered silently in the back of the car. Mom and Dad were also silent in the front.

After the car was parked and the four of them stood in the driveway, Wolf, the butler came smoothly out the front door.

"Welcome," Wolf said, in his usual overly polite way. He stood in a way that offered the family the polite instruction to move on into the mansion.

Inside, Ramsey came down the stairs with a loud welcome.

"Hello! Hello!" He said, moving toward Mom and Dad with his arms out. Hugs happened all around before he finally turned to Milo and Meg.

"Kids," he said, "what do you like to eat for lunch?"

"I don't know. Tacos?" Milo said.

Ramsey turned to Wolf. "Do we have..."

"I'm afraid we're all out of tacos." Wolf said, in what Milo and Meg thought was a comically polite tone of voice. "Might I offer Cream of mushroom soup? Or perhaps, as an alternate selection - "

"Pizza!" Ramsey interrupted Wolf.

"Pizza sounds good," Meg said happily.

Wolf turned to Ramsey, never losing his ultra-polite manner, and asked, "Shall I order pizza for delivery, sir?"

"Yes," Ramsey answered. "Pizza delivery! Nothing but the best!"

Boredom began to settle on Milo and Meg as they waited for the pizza. Mom and Mr. Ramsey began working together on some paperwork that seemed like the real reason they were here today. It turned out that Mr. Ramsey was on the verge of leaving the country for three months, to vacation on a private island he owned. For whatever reason, a bunch of boring papers had to be signed before he left on his vacation.

Dad had struck up a conversation with Wolf, of all people, and as far as Milo and Meg could tell, they talked about absolutely nothing with an amazing amount of enthusiasm.

Meg caught Milo staring up the stairway. She leaned in close so they could speak without anyone else hearing.

"We're not going to get inside any of those locked rooms today."

"I know, I know I just wish…"

"What are the chances of Phoebe being part of this house, anyway?" Meg asked.

"No, none," said Milo. "I just want to know for sure."

Finally the pizza arrived, and everyone gathered around a large table.

"Honestly," Mom, said, "What is it like to own your own island?"

Ramsey cleared his throat. "It's beautiful," he began. "The beach curves exactly like a crescent moon, and the sand! The sand is the whitest, most brilliant sand in the world."

Mom and Dad shook their heads in happy disbelief.

"But if you ask me," Ramsey continued, "I would trade it all back in an instant."

"Trade it for what?" Dad asked.

"Forgive me for being a bit sentimental," Ramsey began, "but I would trade it in an instant, in exchange for a simpler time."

"Well, wouldn't we all love to return to a simpler time?" Mom said, supportively.

"Anyway," Ramsey said, pulling himself out of his sentimental moment, "Kids, how's the pizza? Does it meet your approval?"

"Sure does," said Meg.

"Mhmm," moaned Milo, unable to open his pizza-filled mouth.

The conversation turned bland, as the business of the day was done, and everyone enjoyed the pizza.

Hands were shaken, hugs were exchanged, and all the goodbye pleasantries spoken. Milo and

Meg climbed back in the back seat, Mom and Dad into the front, and the car moved slowly toward the large front gate. Milo watched as the gate swung open gracefully. Dad moved the car through the opening.

On the way through Milo happened to look toward the mail box half hidden in the leaves of a large tree. The name on the mail box said "Ramsey," in bold letters. Then, just as the car was pulling past it, he saw another name. It was stenciled on the gate itself, half-hidden by vines and leaves. His eyes opened wide. The car was pulling fast away. Milo turned back and squinted. The car was out on the street now and the large gate was closing behind them. Milo turned to Meg. She knew he had seen something important, but she also knew he had to be careful blurting out whatever it was.

Her look silently asked him "What?"

He leaned in to Meg's ear and whispered, "The name on the gate."

Meg looked at him, this time with a confused expression.

He leaned in and whispered again. "It says 'Phoebe,' on the gate. I had to look a second time, because it's half covered by vines."

Meg twisted her head to piece the news together.

"Mom," Meg said.

"Yes?"

"When is Mr. Ramsey leaving on his vacation?"

"Oh, he's getting on a plane right away. That's why we had to do this over lunch."

Meg nodded. She looked at Milo, who grimaced back at her. Once again, they faced roadblocks they didn't know how to get past.

"Are we still grounded?" Meg asked, knowing the answer.

"Of course you're still grounded," Mom said. "All weekend."

13

Meg tossed the tennis ball at the ceiling.

"Phoebe," she said.

Milo caught the ball and tossed it back at the ceiling. "Who the heck is this person, anyway?" He asked.

Meg threw the tennis ball toward the corner of the wall, where it bounced off the floor, off the wall, and came back to her.

"We're grounded," she said. "We can't even visit Icarus again until Monday morning. Ramsey's gone on a three month vacation, so we can't go ask him about this. What can we do?"

Milo sat on the edge of the bed and tapped his foot on the floor.

"I don't know. I mean, Ramsey can't be the artist, can he? Is that even possible?"

"Anything's possible," Meg said absently, throwing the ball off-the-floor, off-the-wall, and bouncing back into her hand.

Around 2 O'clock Sunday afternoon, a very bored Meg knocked on Milo's door.

"Yeah," Milo called from inside.

Meg opened the door and casually walked in carrying a drawing notebook.

"Whatchu been up to?" Milo asked, still lying flat on his bed.

Meg sat on the corner of the bed and sighed.

"I've been drawing," she said. She flipped through a few pages of the notebook and shook her head. "I don't know why. I can't even draw the way Phoebe draws Icarus."

Milo sat up and scooted toward his sister. "Let me see," he said.

Meg handed the notebook to him. "Just don't be too honest if you hate it."

Milo flipped through the pages. He stopped to inspect one drawing. He flipped to the next one without saying anything.

Meg watched him flip the page over. She cleared her throat.

Milo gave the notebook back without saying anything. He looked away at nothing in particular.

"Well?" Meg asked.

"Hm? What?"

"Any thoughts on my drawings?"

"Oh, that," Milo said adjusting his sitting position a little. "You said not to be honest if I hated it."

Meg punched him in the shoulder.

They both laughed.

"It's good," he finally said.

"I was thinking, while I was drawing, " Meg began. "This is sort of crazy, isn't it. We are able to enter a world that is drawn and painted. We're trying to find the Artist who creates it. Why are we trying to find the Artist outside of his created world? Why shouldn't we be able to find the Artist inside the created world?"

Milo didn't answer right away. He looked down at the floor. "You're saying we should be able to find Phoebe in Icarus?"

Meg suddenly felt unsure of herself.

"I don't know," she said. "It seemed like a good idea when I thought it."

Milo gave his sister a look. "We have to go in before school tomorrow morning," he said.

Meg nodded. "Yeah," she said casually.

They spent the rest of Sunday sitting around lazily until their parents called them to come down and eat some dinner.

What would they find the next morning, they both wondered? Should they be in Icarus right now, helping out with whatever was going on now? Yes, they both felt. They were losing time. What would happen to Nannette and Wolf while they were gone?

Milo and Meg could only hope that Nanette and Wolf were okay.

15

Monday morning was a little more stressful than usual for both Milo and Meg.

As soon as she woke up, Milo remembered that he should have been spending the weekend writing a paper for Biology class. It was due today, and he'd spent this whole weekend forgetting about it.

Milo and Meg's mom was rushing them to get ready, since she and Dad had to leave earlier than normal, so she could meet a client for breakfast.

"Come on, come on, we have to be out of this house," Mom kept nagging.

"Mom, we walk to school! Why can't we leave after you?"

"We have to make sure the security system is turned on," Mom said.

"So…teach us how to set the alarm. What's wrong? You think Milo and I are too dumb to remember a code?"

"Watch that mouth of yours, Meg, unless you want to stay grounded for the rest of the week."

Milo gave Meg the usual look, a mix of admiration and worry.

Finally everyone was out the front door.

"See you tonight, sweeties!" Mom shouted as she ran to the driver's door of the car.

Dad - who wanted Milo and Meg to know that he 'understood' - opened the passenger door and gave them both a smile. "Stay focused today," he advised. "I believe in both of you."

Meg let out a sarcastic laugh.

Milo elbowed her as a caution.

Dad turned his face sideways. "See you after school," he said, and sat down in the car.

The car doors slammed shut and the parents drove away.

As soon as the car turned the corner and was out of sight, Milo and Meg began running down the street toward the park.

16

When they reached the two trees at the top of the hill, Milo did not hesitate. Squeezing between the trees had become second nature to him by now.

A second later he was inside.

Meg followed quickly.

They stood motionless.

Icarus was quiet.

Together Milo and Meg - once again drawings, but with watercolor painted clothes and backpacks on - looked up at the trees, down at the bushes and undergrowth, and out at the distance. All was quiet, surprisingly quiet.

Milo turned all the way around, listening intently for any sound.

He jumped slightly when a bird squawked and flew from a branch in the tree above him.

Meg watched the bird fly away. It had the usual watercolor markings of bright red tips on its wings, a green underbelly, and a deep blue crest on its head.

Neither of them said anything.

After a couple minutes they began walking.

They didn't need to tell each other where they were going. At this point, it was shared instinct. They were heading in the direction of Nanette's hut.

Would Nanette's hut even be standing, they wondered.

They walked with a sense of worry, though. Something did not feel right.

Each fallen tree trunk they stepped over, every hanging branch they had to push away, all felt like something was missing.

Even with the occasional bird flapping above them, things just felt too quiet.

They continued walking, though.

They slowed down as they neared the area of Nanette's hut. They couldn't see it, but they were close. Everything was eerily silent.

Milo stopped walking and held his arm out to signal Meg to stop also.

Not really sure why he was doing it, Milo crouched down.

Together, Milo and Meg listened. They strained their ears for any of the regular sounds, for any unusual sound, for any clue to the strange feeling they both shared.

Nothing.

Maybe they were worried about nothing.

Still crouching, they moved ahead. They climbed over a fallen tree trunk.

They stepped awkwardly through some undergrowth. Then they saw the hut. It was all there. There was no sign that it had been burned in a Gort attack.

They stopped.

Nothing stirred.

No smoke billowed out of the chimney.

Nanette and Wolf did not seem to be there.

Then Milo and Meg each breathed a panicked breath as two cold, clammy, boney Gort hands covered each of their mouths.

"Quiet!" a voice said, sounding oddly calm and demanding at the same time.

Meg looked at her brother with wide open, panicked eyes.

Neither of them could see the Gort. As they looked at each other, though, they could see the boney hand holding the other's mouth.

"Relax," the voice said. Meg had never heard a Gort speak before, but she thought that the voice sounded female.

A moment passed. It was only a second or two, but it felt to Milo and Meg like many minutes.

They actually did relax a little bit.

"I am not your enemy," the voice said.

This managed to relax Milo and Meg slightly more.

Finally the boney hands pulled away from each of them, and Milo and Meg were able to look up at their visitor.

It was a Gort, alright.

The angled, sharp head looked down at them. The face looked thoughtful and compassionate.

"Yes, I am what you call a 'Gort,'" the creature said. I have left my tribe. I am alone, and I think I can help you.

Meg looked at Milo, unsure what to do.

"What do you want from us?" Milo asked.

"Nothing," said the Gort.

"Why are you here?" Meg asked. "Why did you leave your tribe?"

"I have questions," the Gort said. "I do not think I believe everything I am told. I disagreed with them. So I was sentenced. I escaped. Now I am on the run."

"What should we call you? "Milo asked.

"I am Dreena."

Meg let out a relieved breath. "Do you know Nanette and Wolf?" She asked

"I know who they are, but I have not talked to them. They would not trust me like you might. Thank you for believing me."

Milo looked at Dreena. She had wings that spread out from her back naturally. When she relaxed, the wings seemed to close onto her back almost like they weren't even there.

"What do you want?" Meg asked. "What is your plan?"

Dreena looked down and sighed. "Something is wrong with Icarus," she said. "The Artist has not finished creating us. Mysteries surround us. We need answers, and I do not believe the answers we have been told."

"What do you know about The Artist?" Milo asked.

"I know where she lives."

"She..." Meg looked at Milo, then back to Dreena. "Is it Phoebe?" Meg asked.

"Yes," Dreena said quietly.

Meg did not understand everything that was happening. She turned to Dreena. "Can we go to Nanette's hut? Can we see if Nanette and Wolf are there? We can promise them you are trustworthy."

Dreena looked up at Meg. "I have not seen anyone in the hut," she said. "I think they are not there."

Milo stood slowly. He looked across the clearing at the hut.

Meg was slower to stand. She looked behind them, into the trees and undergrowth. Then she turned her gaze to the hut.

"I think she's right," Milo said. "No one home."

Meg turned to Dreena. "Do you think you are being followed?" she asked.

"They are hunting for me, no doubt," Dreena said. "I am sure I have lost them for now, but I must keep moving."

Milo took a step forward and said, "Let's make sure."

He lifted his foot over a stump and stepped into the small clearing. He walked toward the hut, looking left and right as he went.

Meg followed.

Dreena waited until Milo and Meg had reached the hut, then unfurled her wings and quickly flew across the clearing, landing silently next to Meg.

Milo peered in the window.

"Nobody home," he sighed.

The three of them stood together, wondering what to do next.

"We will go see Phoebe," Dreena said.

"We can see her? Can we meet and talk to her?," Meg asked.

Dreena turned slowly to Meg. "Phoebe lives here in Icarus," she said.

Meg twisted her face toward Milo.

"Where?" asked Milo.

"She lives up there." Dreena looked away toward the mountain. Milo and Meg followed her gaze.

"Up there?" Meg looked from the mountain back to Dreena.

"Up there," Dreena replied.

They all looked at each other with a collective thought.

"Can you take us there?" Milo asked.

Dreena nodded. "Yes, we have a long journey. We should begin."

Meg gave Milo a sarcastic look. "Is this your way of getting out of Biology class?"

"This won't get me out of Biology. It'll still be the start of the day whenever we get back."

"Sounds to me like we're going to be in Icarus for a long time," Meg said.

"I guess we'll find out if this time thing works over long periods."

Meg shook her head at Milo and smiled.

Dreena stretched a boney finger between Milo and Meg. "We should begin our journey. I fear that my people are getting close."

"Okay," Meg said.

Dreena moved smoothly to the right side of Nanette's hut and disappeared into thick bushes. Milo followed and Meg rolled her eyes before finally stepping through the bushes herself.

Meg instantly knew they were in a deeper, darker part of the forest than they had ever been in before.

It also felt colder.

Meg struggled to keep up with the pace Dreena and Milo were moving at. Finally she caught up with Milo, but he had also lost Dreena.

They stopped.

Where was she?

Then Dreena's calming voice came from a thicket next to them.

"I have to be stealthy," Dreena said, catching Milo and Meg off guard. "Sometimes you will not see me. Sometimes I may move faster than you can. Sometimes I have to hide for my own safety. If you do not see me, or feel you have lost me, stop and be still. This is the best advice I can give you."

Dreena emerged from the thicket and smiled at them - if you can call twisting her angled, boney face toward them smiling.

"Let's continue," she said, and moved quickly ahead of them again.

Meg turned and walked alongside Milo. "What have we gotten into this time?" she asked, not expecting an answer.

After what seemed like an hour of walking, Dreena, Meg, and Milo had begun climbing. They were on the mountainside now, and the path they were walking on was sloped upward at a sharp angle.

Meg breathed heavily as she climbed up behind Dreena and Milo. Her legs began to feel like rubber. She wanted nothing more than to sit down and have a tall cool glass of water.

Dreena kept walking, though. Milo kept up with Dreena's pace. Meg plodded along behind them, climbing, climbing, up, up, higher and higher.

Finally Dreena stopped.

They had reached a clearing that allowed them to turn back and look down where they had come from.

The valley below them was beautiful.

Dreena moved back behind a tree, fearing for her safety.

Milo stared at the scene in front of him.

"It's beautiful," he said to Meg.

Meg nodded silently.

She turned around and arched her neck upward. She could see part of a house quite a ways further up. It was partly hidden by trees, but she could clearly see the wooden corner and wall of a house.

"Is that where we're going?" Meg asked.

Dreena poked her head from the tree she was hiding behind and arched her neck in the direction Meg was looking.

"Yes," Dreena said. "Come."

Dreena began climbing again.

Milo breathed a heavy breath, exhaled, and began climbing after Dreena.

Meg wanted to take a break. She wanted to sit. She wanted to take in the beauty of the valley below them.

She had no choice, though. She did not want to be left alone in this world. She began walking, climbing. Quickly, she ran upwards towards Milo. She caught up with him, and fell into the rhythm of movement behind him.

After another half-hour they finally reached the house on the side of the mountain.

Dreena did not hesitate. She glided up to the door and knocked.

A silent moment passed before the door opened.

A woman opened and looked out the door at them. She was young. Meg guessed she looked about 20 years old. She had beautiful brown hair, and a calm accepting expression.

"Hello, Dreena," the woman said.

"Hello, Phoebe. I have brought friends."

Dreena stepped aside and let Milo and Meg look directly at the woman.

"Welcome," she said. "Come in. Sit and rest your tired legs. You have been walking for so long."

Meg took a step forward and stopped. She wasn't sure if this new, strange house was safe.

She had no choice, she realized, and decided to trust Dreena, and step inside.

Milo followed.

The house was humble. The furniture was old and faded. The walls were painted white, but with many darker, faded areas.

The woman closed the door after everyone had stepped inside.

"Welcome to my house," she said. "I am Phoebe."

An awkward silence settled on them. Finally Meg said, "Hi, thanks. It's a pleasure to meet you. I'm Meg."

"And I'm Milo. I'm just glad we made it up the side of this mountain."

"Yes." Phoebe motioned for them to sit. "What would you like? Tea? Juice? I have muffins to eat, if you are hungry."

Together,  Milo and Meg moved to two chairs and sat down.

"Muffins sound good," Milo blurted, giving away his hunger.

"And something to drink?" Phoebe asked.

"Tea," Meg said.

"Yeah, I'll have tea," said Milo.

Phoebe left for the kitchen. Dreena squeezed her limbs together tightly and settled onto a couch that faced Milo and Meg.

"You know Phoebe," Meg said to Dreena, more as a question than as a comment.

"We met a few days ago," Dreena said, offering no further information.

Several minutes passed as quiet rattling noises came from the kitchen. Milo and Meg were happy enough just to sit.

Finally Phoebe returned from the kitchen with cups on saucers.

"I hope you like the tea," Phoebe said. "I don't know how similar it is to tea in your world."

Meg once again found herself watching the pencil line of steam drawing itself up out of the cup.

"And muffins for each of you," Phoebe said, setting down a plate.

Phoebe sat on the couch next to Dreena, let out a relaxed breath, and looked across at Milo and Meg.

"Well," she said, smiling at them, "what did you want to see me about?"

Milo took a bite of a muffin, marveled silently at how delicious it was, and glanced over at his sister.

"Well…" Milo cleared his throat and drank a sip of tea. "We, um, we wanted to find the artist who is drawing and painting all of this."

Phoebe gave Milo a calming and supportive look. "And because you have seen my name, you want to talk to me about this."

Milo looked at her, slightly confused. "Um, I mean, is that, does that make sense?"

"I suppose it does," Phoebe said. "But I am not The Artist."

This time even Dreena looked at Phoebe with surprise.

Phoebe could see that they were confused. "Let me tell you something that will answer your questions."

Meg sipped her tea. Milo swallowed a bite of muffin. Dreena twisted her boney limbs sideways so she could face Phoebe more directly.

"Do you know Ramsey Fisher?" Phoebe asked.

Milo choked on some tea, and accidentally spit a little tea spray out of his mouth.

Meg laughed. "Smooth, Milo. Very smooth."

"Shut up," Milo said, smiling but embarrassed.

Phoebe leaned forward and let out a calming breath.

"Ramsey Fisher," Phoebe said, looking deeply emotional, "is my brother."

No one knew what to say. A curious silence filled the room.

"You see…" Phoebe looked around the room at them. She stood up and moved to the window at the far end of the room.

She turned back from the window. "I am no longer alive."

This time, Dreena saved Milo and Meg from finding the right question.

"How is it," Dreena began, "that you are here talking to us?"

Phoebe moved slowly back toward them. She looked directly at Meg. "You are right to be looking for The Artist. You are very clever, both of you," she said, looking from Meg to Milo. "I was Ramsey's older sister. We grew up three years apart. Through our teens all I did was draw and paint. It seemed certain that I would be an artist for the rest of my life. We were very close, Ramsey and I. As brother and sister we seemed to understand each other in ways that no one else could."

Phoebe paused. Milo, Meg, and Dreena were rapt with attention.

"When I tragically passed away at the age of 20, I think it left a hole in my brother's heart. Bless his soul, he has spent his whole life trying to keep my memory alive."

Phoebe picked up her own tea cup, looked sadly into the cup, and looked back up at her guests.

"I originally created this world of Icarus. It is Ramsey, though, who keeps it alive. He draws for me, to keep me alive. I used to be The Artist. Now it is my brother Ramsey who is The Artist."

Phoebe stopped talking.

Dreena looked at Phoebe with deep empathy.

Milo slowly took another bite of his muffin, lost in new thought.

Meg leaned back in her chair and sipped her tea.

"So…" Meg said, "Ramsey creates Icarus because you first created it as a teenager?"

Phoebe nodded.

"And he has your name 'Phoebe' on his house, in honor of you?"

"Yes," Phoebe said.

"So was Nanette originally your creation? And Wolf?"

This time Phoebe paused before answering.

"You can say I created Nanette, although so many years have passed that my brother Ramsey has begun to build some of his own creations. He has taken it further than I ever could have. I never drew Wolf. That is all my brother's creation."

Milo saw where his sister was going with this, and picked up where she had stopped. "Does Ramsey understand that Nanette and Wolf, and their other friends from their village, feel that The Artist, that Ramsey, doesn't understand them? That they think and feel, as living creatures?"

"I understand it," Phoebe said. "For, here I am, thinking, feeling, talking to you." Does Ramsey understand it? I think he does, but maybe we can do a better job of reminding him."

18

An hour later they were climbing back down the side of the mountain. They walked in silence, stunned by the new world of information they had learned.

Dreena seemed even more nervous this time. She flew as close to the trees as she could.

She knew something.

Then Milo saw it!

A Gort flew across a ravine in front of them.

Then another.

Dreena whispered urgently for Milo and Meg to come toward her under the trees.

They hurried over to her.

"You will have to continue without me," she said, a note of worry in her voice. "You will have to stay off the main path also. Continue down the mountain, but take this alternate path through the forest. I am sorry. I have to leave now."

And she was gone before Milo and Meg could even say goodbye to her.

Meg looked out between the tree branches and saw four Gorts flying quickly away.

"I think she's taking them off our trail," Meg said.

Milo followed Meg's look out through the trees. "She's risking her own life so we'll be okay."

"What should we do?"

Milo gulped. "I think we should do what she said. Keep walking down this mountain."

Meg thought for a moment, and then nodded.

Slowly they stood and turned.

They began walking, heavy with worry for Dreena.

19

Milo and Meg emerged from the forest onto a flat field with a stream running through it.

On the other side of the stream was a small village. At first they were worried who might be in the village, but the sounds coming from the small huts were happy sounds.

"That kind of looks like Nanette's hut," Milo said.

"Yeah," said Meg, "except there are fifteen of them, and they all look alike."

Then they saw someone that looked familiar.

"Is that - " Meg didn't even finish her question.

"Wolf!" Milo shouted.

"And Nanette!"

They began running to a small stone bridge across the stream.

Nanette and Wolf smiled as they approached. Also smiling were the 20 or so others gathering behind Nanette and Wolf.

Meg was first to reach Nanette. They stretched their arms toward each other and hugged a big happy hug. Milo reached for Wolf's hand and they shook hands happily.

"Thanks to the two of you," Nanette said, "here we all are."

"The two of us?" Milo asked. "What did we do?"

"I sure as heck don't know," Nanette answered, "but here we are, all together."

Meg looked at those gathered near them. "Who's - "

"Oh! Let me introduce my sister Janice," Nanette said, proudly.

Janice - looking just enough like Nanette that you could see the family resemblance - stepped up next to her sister.

"Hello," she said calmly.

"Pleased to meet you," Meg said, offering a hand.

Janice grasped Meg's hand and patted it. "I hope you have forgiven my sister for her, well, what should we call it?"

"What?" Nanette interrupted. "You mean my honesty and common sense?"

Janice looked directly into Meg's eyes and gave her a knowing wink. "Sure Nanette. Your honesty and common sense."

Meg gave Janice a smile back. She knew why Janice had given her the wink.

"Well," Nanette barked. "This requires a celebration! Our village is back! Milo and Meg are here. Janice and Wolfy are here. Let's celebrate!"

Everyone turned and happily danced and walked into the center of the small village.

"How did this all happen?" Milo asked Wolf, as they walked.

"We thought you knew," Wolf said. "Did you not find The Artist?"

Milo looked at Wolf with a sideways look. "Did we?" he asked himself. "Maybe we did."

"Well, it sure seems like you did," Wolf said.

The villagers danced and sang and ate delicious food for what seemed like hours.

Milo and Meg were delirious, with happiness and full stomachs, when the party was finally winding down.

Several of the villagers gave Nanette and Wolf hugs before leaving for their own huts.

Milo sat on a bench in front of Nanette's hut.

Meg leaned lazily against a porch railing.

"I think we're about to find out if this time thing still works," Meg said to her brother.

"Oh, sheesh! Biology!"

Meg laughed a little as Milo dropped his head into his hands.

As Milo and Meg stepped out from the two trees, back into the town of August, they saw Clarence and Jackson walking along the street toward school.

"Milo! Meg!" Clarence yelled from the street.

"Hey!" Milo said, as he and Meg walked down the hill toward the street.

"You do your Biology this weekend?" Clarence asked.

"No,"Milo said. "Thanks for reminding me."

"What?"

"Let's talk about something else," Milo said jokingly.

"What time is it?" asked Meg.

Clarence looked at his watch. "It's almost 8," he said. "We're going to be late."

Meg and Milo gave each other a knowing look as the four of them headed down the street toward school. Time hadn't passed. That whole climb up the mountainside, the hour with Phoebe, the climb back down, the village party with Nannette and Wolf, none of it had altered time back here in August.

Clarence and Jackson walked in front. Milo and Meg fell in behind them.

"I'm tired," Milo said.

"Tired!" Clarence turned around and looked at Milo. "What, you stay up late playing video games or something?"

Milo laughed and said, "Yeah, something like that."

They turned the corner and saw the school up ahead.

"You're going to regret not doing your Biology," Clarence said.

"Yes," replied Milo, "I sure am. Thanks for making me feel like a failure."

They climbed a few of the concrete steps toward the front of the school.

Meg tried to speak quietly, so only Milo could hear her. "What ever happened to Dreena?" she asked.

"Who's Dreena?" Clarence blurted out, before Milo could even answer.

"Someone we met this weekend," Milo said.

They continued up the steps toward the school's main doorway.

"Yeah," Milo said to Meg, thoughtfully. "What did happen to Dreena?"

Clarence turned back from the top of the steps. "You two are going to have to fill us in on what you're talking about."

"Maybe after school," Milo said. "We're going to be late."

And they all turned toward the school entrance, starting what seemed to almost everyone like another normal day in the town of August.